The Lavender Mud Fairy

by Linda P. Geiger

Miracle Moments Press

Lakewood, Colorado

Also by Linda P. Geiger (a.k.a. Linda P. Voyles):

Simply Successful Surgery: Secrets to Faster Healing

The Lavender Mud Fairy

Copyright © 2016 by Linda P. Geiger

Miracle Moments Press
an imprint of Miracles Every Moment Publishing
Lakewood, Colorado
www.MiraclesEveryMoment.com

Illustrations by Taeseok Yoon

Editing, design, and production by Jan Allegretti
www.ListenToTheSilence.com

ISBN: 978-0-9791413-4-8

To Brandon
with much love from Nana

Special thanks to Isla Rose
for her magical inspiration

Chapter 1

A Mysterious Light

There once was a beautiful, sweet, tiny fairy named Liddya, who lived at the bottom of an old, dark, deserted rabbit hole at the edge of a meadow. The mouth of the rabbit hole was near a wild raspberry patch, and was hidden by an overgrown juniper bush.

Little Liddya, with her tiny blonde curls, was happy and content, flittering and twittering about the chambers of her tiny home, day after day. Her lavender fairy gown sparkled, even in the darkness of the shadowy rabbit hole. You see, the fabric of the fairy gown had a shimmer all its own, with tiny magical threads of light woven all through it. So Liddya glowed wherever she went, lighting her way with each little flutter of her wings, flitting here and there all day long.

If you looked closely, you could also see a cluster of tiny sparkling stars that swirled all around her, stars that belonged only to Liddya. They joyfully swirled in the glowing breezes of her flight, never leaving her side, dancing in the air like diamonds in the night sky. The little stars were happy, too. There were five of them, and they were all Liddya's friends.

There was Sparkle, a pretty little silvery gold star who was so wise, she always knew just what to do. The other stars looked up to her, and they often asked her about things, like why stars are shiny while rocks and dirt are not. And Sparkle would answer them with important information. They needed to learn that stars are meant to shine, she'd tell them, because that is what stars love to do.

Glo was a tiny star who worked very hard. She loved to clean and scrub and cook and sew. She made little shimmery curtains for Liddya's rooms, and yummy creamy soups and polka dotted candy sticks. Liddya's sparkly gown with shimmery shiny threads was one of Glo's best creations. But her favorite thing to do was to change the colors of things with her magical painting star tip. You see, that particular star tip was like no other—it could wiggle and fizzle until it turned things into different colors. She would make Liddya's little kitchen all purple one day...and the next day she would turn it to yellow and pink stripes!

Little Twinkle stayed in the background most of the time. She liked to spend most of the day up near the ceiling, where she could just be quiet and watch the others. When any of the stars or Liddya would invite her to tea, or to play twiddly-widdly-winks, Twinkle's teeny star face would turn rosy pink and she would turn her face away and wait until they forgot about her again. The truth was she really loved it when they asked, but it was so very scary to think of trying to learn a new game or sip tea out of a delicate tiny cup. What if she did it wrong? Or broke the cup? What then?! So instead, she quietly imagined that someday she would be queen of all the stars, and have tea with all her royal court with silver sparkly tea sets and tiny real sugar lumps that she would know very well how to stir into her tea. She would be so very fine someday. But not today, she thought. Not today.

Spike was a bossy star. He had a prickly shiny collar that he liked to wear sometimes to show the others how strong and powerful he was. He often argued with Sparkle about why stars shine. He told Glo how to sew, and he teased Twinkle about her rosy cheeks. Sometimes he even told Liddya that he was not going to help with the fairy jobs they all shared. Fairy jobs were fun things like practicing musical twittering, magically moving the little table and chairs around the house to make clouds of glistening fairy dust...things like that. Spike was the best at moving the furniture. Because he was so strong, it was easy for him to swirl it around and around, stirring up great big clouds of fairy dust. But sometimes he just wouldn't. Sparkle and Liddya seemed not to notice how bossy and stubborn he was. But the others sometimes chattered about it in the corner before they went to their teensy tiny star beds at the end of the day.

And then there was Stella. Stella believed that Liddya was actually and truly her servant. After all, Stella was the most beautiful golden star in the rabbit hole! And Liddya was only a silly fairy. None of the others seemed to know about Stella's amazing beauty and wit, though Stella couldn't imagine how they could possibly be with her each day and not notice. It was so very clear to Stella. Each day, after Liddya arose and got herself ready for the day and was finally out of Stella's way, Stella would settle into Liddya's bed, pull up the covers just so, and wait for the others to serve her. Sometimes Glo would bring Stella her breakfast. Usually Sparkle would just shake her little star head at her. Spike liked to stand on the headboard and shout orders! He really admired the beautiful Stella, so he helped her whenever he could. He always tried to make sure the others knew what she wanted, and hoped that someday she would notice how handsome and strong he was.

They were silly stars. They were Liddya's friends. They had a wonderful little life in the old deserted rabbit hole.

ONE DAY, LIDDYA SAT AND THOUGHT, and then she thought some more. While she was thinking, her eyes wandered around the rabbit hole, her little round lovely home. Suddenly she noticed a light she had never seen before, high up toward the ceiling. She took a closer look, and saw there was a tunnel she had never noticed before...and it led straight to the light way up high!

"How exciting!" she thought. "Why in the world did I not notice this before? I simply must go explore it!"

And with that thought, she lifted and flittered up and up and up through the tunnel, her sparkling starlit magical shimmering fairy gown lighting the way toward the little round light way up high. The closer she flew to the brightness, the bigger it seemed to get. Her little star friends flew quietly behind her, hiding from the strange bright light.

Finally Liddya reached the end of the tunnel, and discovered something truly amazing. "My, oh my!" she thought, as she put her tiny hands over her mouth. The small round light opened out into a beautiful sunlit meadow with green grasses waving softly in the breeze, and red and yellow and purple wildflowers all dancing about in the wind. The meadow was bordered by tall pine trees all standing in rows, as though their only job was to guard the meadow day and night.

Liddya felt a wave of wonderment as she thought of how much fun it would be just to fly and fly out over the beautiful meadow! So she decided to do just that, for she had never had so much room to fly and twitter about in her tiny home. She imagined taking off and flying all around the meadow as fast as she could go. She was so excited to have this endless space all to herself—it would be the most fun ever!

But just as she sprang off the ground to begin her amazing adventurous flight—

THUMP! BAM!

"Oooh, what...happened?!" she thought slowly. Her little head felt like it was in a foggy grey cloud. She couldn't see very well. It was dark all around her except for her shimmering gown, and some of her star friends swirling slowly next to her.

So she tried to think, and thought some more. "Where am I?" she wondered.

And as she thought, she began to see the blurry walls of her little rabbit hole. Somehow she had fallen back inside and all the way down the tunnel into her little home. Some of her stars had been knocked down, too, and were lying on the dirt beside her. Liddya tapped Twinkle and Glo gently to see if they were okay. Slowly they began to move a little and a little more, and finally, though weakly, they were dizzily swirling around her again. Spike's collar had been knocked off, and Stella was twirling around in a bit of a tizzy, very upset to be treated in such a rough and surprising manner. Sparkle sat quietly and watched the others, trying to figure out what had just happened to them all.

As Liddya's eyes began to focus, she spotted the light way up there in the ceiling and remembered what she had set out to do. Now more than ever, she wanted to make her way up to that light at the end of the tunnel and go flying all around that beautiful meadow. So she shook out her fairy wings and hopped up toward the light, through the long tunnel to the mouth of the rabbit hole—and promptly fell back to the ground instead...again!

"Ow!" she thought. "My head really hurts. I guess I don't want to fly again if it's going to hurt my head so much." So she glided slowly to her tiny fairy bed to take a nap, followed by her tiny friends, who snuggled in to their teensy tiny star beds—all except Sparkle, that is. She was too worried about Liddya and her tiny star friends after the thumping and bumping they'd taken, so she promised to keep watch over all of them through the night.

Chapter 2

Lumps and Bumps in the Meadow

When Liddya woke up the next morning, her very first thought was that she wanted to go see that beautiful meadow again! So off she flew, up and up and up through the tunnel. This time she slowed down near the entrance, still remembering her mysterious fall back down into the tunnel the day before, and the aching headache it had given her. Liddya's shimmering stars paused with her, as though they, too, were afraid.

But when the tiny fairy reached the opening, she didn't just notice the beautiful meadow with its colorful dancing wildflowers. This time her attention went straight to a HUGE lumpy bumpy rabbit sitting in the raspberry patch right outside the entryway of the rabbit hole! He was bigger than anything she had ever seen.

"My, oh my!" she thought.

Liddya was glad to see that the rabbit was clearly way too big to fit through the rabbit hole tunnel. He was enormous! And he was very lumpy. Liddya thought for a while. She watched as the rabbit slowly worked at hopping his lumpy bumpy rabbit body from berry bush to berry bush. She wondered what lumpy bumpy rabbits liked to do. From what she could see, it seemed they liked to twitch their whiskered noses and hop. "What a very strange creature," she thought, "and very large!"

Just then the lumpy bumpy rabbit spotted Liddya watching him, and he stared at her with a furry whiskery scowl. He did not seem very friendly at all.

"Oh well," Liddya thought. "Forget about him. I would rather fly than hop." And with a little flutter, she got in position to begin her wonderful flight around the meadow. But before she knew it, with just one tiny movement, that lumpy bumpy rabbit in the raspberry patch hopped one very giant hop toward her.

THUMP! BAM!

...and once again Liddya found herself waking up at the bottom of the tunnel with a foggy cloudy achy head, and her stunned and frightened little fairy stars lying on the dirt floor beside her.

"Oh my, oh my. This just will not do!" she thought. "Now I know why we keep ending up back at the bottom of the tunnel. But why, oh why does that lumpy bumpy rabbit want to thump me? Why is he so grumpy?! That bad lumpy bumpy rabbit! That very mean ol' lumpy rabbit!"

Liddya fussed and fumed in her little fairy house, all the while wishing she could be outside flying around and around the beautiful meadow. But she just didn't know what to do about that mean ol' thumping bumping rabbit, so she decided to go to bed to rest her achy head. The last thing she saw as she drifted off to sleep was Sparkle resting in her teensy star bed with one little starry eye open, determined to watch over Liddya all night long.

THE NEXT DAY, the tiny shiny lavender fairy with all her shimmering sparkly stars flew once again to the top of the rabbit hole. This time, when Liddya got to the entrance she stayed very still, looking for the lumpy bumpy rabbit. As her tiny fairy eyes scanned the raspberry patch, it began to rain. One by one, big fat drops of rain came down, dropping and plopping on the dirt near the entry to the rabbit hole, plop plop plop, again and again. Soon the rain came down even harder, and more and more raindrops fell in the dirt.

And then she spotted him. "Oh, no!" thought Liddya. "There's the rabbit!" He was hiding under a leaf of the nearby umbrella tree, holding very still and staying very dry as the raindrops dropped and plopped all around him. When Liddya saw him she felt a shiver of fear, and her star friends began to twitter nervously around her.

But just then she noticed that the lumpy bumpy rabbit looked sad...his rabbit nose was very still, and his ears no longer stood up—they were drooping down beside him. "Why in the world would a lumpy bumpy rabbit be sad?" she wondered. "Never mind. I just want him to stay away!"

So Liddya backed away from the edge of the tunnel, out of sight of the mean old rabbit, so she could think about what to do. But her star friends were still swirling and twittering about. "Shhh! This time we must not be seen!" she thought as she ducked deeper inside the tunnel. And there she sat, somewhere between the edge of the rabbit hole and her tiny fairy home, deep in thought about that lumpy bumpy rabbit.

Suddenly Liddya noticed that the raindrops had splashed mud all over her shimmering lavender dress. It was soaked in mud! "Oh, no!" she thought. Her gown was dripping with mud, and so were all of the tiny stars, so that their light was now barely glowing at all. Spike and Sparkle were stuck in a mud puddle with Twinkle. Glo and Stella dripped with thick muddy slop. There was no more shimmer to Liddya's gown—the lavender was gone, hidden by the reddish brown muck. "Oh, how sad!" she thought. "My beautiful lavender fairy dress is all covered in mud, and my tiny star friends are all stuck in one spot. If only I could get out of this rabbit hole, the rain might wash the mud away so my lights and stars could shine again...!"

But she had never even been outside the rabbit hole, and had never before considered flying around in the rain. She needed to take a closer look, so she went back up to the top of the tunnel to look out at the meadow. There she saw the rabbit—right at the very top of their rabbit hole! "Oh, no! He's looking right at me with his furry whiskery scowl," Liddya thought. "Quick, what shall I do so he doesn't thump me again?! And why, oh why does he want to thump me all the time?!" She peered over the edge of the tunnel at his scowling face, and wished she wasn't so afraid of him.

The lavender fairy tried to hold very, very still. But her muddy little stars began to twitter again, as it was their nature to do. It was wet and slippery up near the top of the tunnel, and Stella and Glo were trying to get the others unstuck from the mud. "Stop! Oh, Stop!" thought Liddya. "The rabbit will surely see, and he will thump us again!" Very carefully she peeked over the edge of the rabbit hole, and there he was, gazing right in her direction.

But it was a very strange thing. This time the rabbit did not seem to see Liddya at all. And he didn't even see her twittering stars. No, she was quite certain he did not see any of them. How very, very strange it was!

After what seemed like a very long time, Liddya cautiously...slowly...fluttered her wings...but only slightly. She looked right at the lumpy bumpy rabbit, but could not see any sign at all that the mean rabbit could see her. Not at all!

"Could it be," she wondered, "that the mud has made us invisible? It's covered up our glittery shiny light—so maybe that's why he doesn't seem to know we're here."

Liddya tried not to giggle at her good fortune. Maybe—just maybe—this meant she could fly out of her rabbit hole and all around the meadow after all, without ever having to worry about getting thumped by that mean old lumpy rabbit. But how could she be sure? And anyway, who ever heard of a fairy flying around all covered in mud? She was quite sure she never had.

"Hmmm," she thought. "I want so much to fly around the meadow. I wonder...my gown feels heavy with all this mud on it.

Actually, so do my wings. It will probably take some extra energy to fly this way." But Liddya knew deep inside that it was exactly what she would try to do.

So she backed way up into the tunnel until the lumpy bumpy rabbit was completely out of sight. She motioned to her little stars that it was time to get ready, to gather all their energy under the drippy mud. They all got in line, dripping with mud but ready to go. Then all together, the fairy and her stars ran toward the entrance as fast as they could, and jumped as high as they could, and flew right on past that lumpy bumpy rabbit! Out into the rainy meadow they went, past the umbrella leaf, past the wild raspberry patch and up into the sky as fast as they could go. It was just as Liddya had imagined. It was wonderful!

Up and down and around the meadow they flew, the magical lavender fairy and her teensy tiny stars. As they did, the raindrops gave each tiny star a little bath, until they all sparkled even brighter than ever before. And the magical lavender fairy gown began to drip, drip, drip away all the sloppy mud, until its light once again shone brightly, lighting Liddya's way.

As Liddya flew and flew, she glanced down and saw the rabbit looking up at her. "The rabbit must now be able to see me again," she thought, "with my gown all clean and glowing after the rainy bath." She began to worry, thinking about how much her head had hurt when he thumped her. But at this moment she was flying over the meadow, and having such fun. She decided to forget all about it...at least for now.

With a smile on her tiny face, Liddya flew around and around the meadow as the sun came out to shine through the fluffy clouds now scattered across the sky. She flew like the wind, singing and swirling and floating right past the lumpy bumpy rabbit, over and over again. All the rabbit could do was watch her and hop between the leaves from plant to plant, munching his way through the raspberry patch with his lumpy bumpiness. He did try to jump up and catch Liddya each time she flew near him, but he could not reach her. Liddya was so glad the rabbit could not fly! She hoped he would never ever thump her again.

Liddya was so happy! She flew and flew, this way and that, being careful to stay within the border of the tall, safe pine trees that guarded the meadow day and night, as she somehow knew she should do. They were friendly trees. As she flew past them all standing in a row, straight and tall along the borders of the meadow, they all waved their pine branches at her in the breeze and smiled their wise, protective, loving smiles. The magical lavender fairy felt safe, knowing they were watching out for her. She could tell they would always stand tall, even against the strongest stormy winds.

Chapter 3

Too Heavy
to Fly

And that was how Liddya spent the whole day, flying around and around the meadow, enjoying the beautiful colorful flowers, all under the watchful eyes of the tall, protective pine trees. Whenever she flew anywhere near the rabbit, he tried to swat at her with his big rabbit feet, so she steered away from the area around the raspberry patch. She flew and swirled around the beautiful meadow, her stars sparkling and shining, and her magical lavender fairy gown all aglow. Sparkle and Twinkle and Glo flew and twirled with Liddya while Spike and Stella soared above them, everyone enjoying the view over the beautiful grassy meadow. They didn't want to stop.

When Liddya was finally ready to rest for the night, she looked around for the rabbit, but she couldn't see him. She thought he must have grown tired of watching her. Or maybe he had finally lost interest because he could never catch her in flight. But then, as she glided around one last swirling flight over the meadow, she spotted the rabbit all curled up and sleeping under a great big umbrella leaf. Liddya gathered all her star friends around her, and together they went speeding past the lumpy bumpy rabbit, right down the rabbit hole and straight into their cozy beds. What a wonderful way to spend the day!

THE NEXT MORNING when Liddya awoke, she knew she wanted to go flying in the meadow again. But when she stepped out of bed, her tiny toes squished into a pool of mud on the floor of her tiny room.

"Oh, no!" she thought. "The rainstorm must have dripped rain into my house! The floor is all wet. What shall I do?" Well, since she was a fairy and could fly, she just decided to fly about in her little house instead of walking, so she could get herself ready to go to the meadow without muddying her tiny fairy feet.

Once again she flew with her magical lavender gown and sparkling stars swirling about her, up the tunnel to the entrance of the rabbit hole. The sky was blue and the sun was shining brightly. But sure enough, there was that lumpy bumpy rabbit right near the entryway. The mean old rabbit took a giant hop toward Liddya the moment he saw her, looking for all the world like he was about to thump her! Liddya flitted back out of reach and watched as he leaned in toward the entrance of the rabbit hole and watched her very closely, his nose twitching anxiously and wiggling all about.

"He looks like he wants me to stay in the tunnel," Liddya thought. "But why?"

She sat back down, well out of the lumpy bumpy rabbit's reach, and thought and thought, and thought some more. "Maybe it bothered him to see me flying all around the meadow yesterday. Maybe I'm nothing but a bother to the rabbit. Maybe he doesn't even want me to be here at all!"

Liddya sat inside the tunnel and thought about what she should do. "I want to fly in the meadow, but that lumpy bumpy rabbit won't let me out."

Just then she remembered the magical way the mud had made Liddya and her stars invisible to the rabbit the day before, so they could escape. "Hmm," she thought, "being covered up with mud is the secret to getting past that lumpy grumpy rabbit without getting thumped." Her lavender fairy light brightened at the idea...then her shoulders slumped as she thought, "But there's no rain today, so no raindrops will come and splash mud on my shimmering gown." She sighed a great big fairy sigh. "What shall I do?" she thought.

She went back down into her little house, sat down on her bed, and thought some more. As she

26

was thinking, she shook some wet dirt off of her tiny foot. "Yuck, it sure is sloppy in here after that soggy rainstorm yesterday," she thought. And then her light brightened again. "Oh! Of course! I can use this mud on the floor to cover myself and my stars again, so the rabbit cannot see us!"

And so Liddya and her tiny stars played a game, rolling and giggling and playing on the muddy floor until once again the little lights and sparkles were all hidden. All of them were completely covered in mud. There was no glow, no lavender shimmer, and no sparkly starlight, so they were no longer noticeable to the lumpy rabbit in the raspberry patch. No one would notice the little fairy or her stars when they were covered in mud!

Liddya and her mud-dripping stars gathered all their energy and took a long running start to take off up the tunnel, shooting out through the entrance without even looking for the old rabbit. Out she flew into the beautiful meadow. Around and around the meadow she swirled, with her stars flitting all around her.

But soon Liddya began to notice that the mud was really weighing her down. She must have put on too much of it, and this time there was no rain to rinse it off. It was making her tired, flying with all that heavy mud. She noticed that her little star friends were beginning to drag, too.

"What should I do?" she wondered. "Flying around the meadow is so much fun, I really don't want to go home yet. But if I land here, all the way across the meadow, I'll have to walk all the way home. Besides, the mud might start to fall off as I walk—then that lumpy rabbit might see me and thump me again! What shall I do?"

Liddya thought and thought as she flew slowly...and slowly...and even more slowly. "Oh dear," she worried, "what a terrible dilemma. I don't want to land, but I can't stay up here much longer with this heavy gown and drippy muddy stars."

Just then she saw two of the tall sentinel pine trees waving their treetops at her.

"Come here," they waved. "Look!" Their branches were beckoning to her from the far side of the meadow, where they stood side by side. "Come here," they waved again.

Liddya wanted to go to them, but they were at the very edge of the meadow. It seemed so far away. "What could they want to show me?" she wondered. "What could they want me to do?" She was getting scared. She had never been that close to the edge of the meadow. And she was getting so very tired from flying with her heavy load.

But the pine trees kept calling to her. "Come this way. Look over here, little one," they waved. Liddya thought she even heard them whispering to her in the breeze. "We can help you, little fairy. Fly on over here," they seemed to say as they swayed in the wind.

And so, before her wings were just too tired to make another round, she couldn't resist a quick trip to investigate whatever it was the friendly pine trees wanted to show her.

But, oh! As she turned in their direction, Liddya realized she was more tired than she had thought. As she grew closer to the tall pine trees, she began to sink lower and lower in her flight. "Oh no, I'm going to crash!" she thought. "I cannot stay up!" Down and down she swirled, closer and closer to the row of wavering pines. So tired...so tired. "Can't fly anymore," she thought. She was sinking faster and faster, lower and lower.

Just then, as Liddya reached the lower branches of some of the friendly pines, they stepped aside, parting a space between them. Lower and lower she sank. She was going to hit the ground! "Oh, help!" she thought. "What shall I do?!"

Whooosh—kersplash! Blub, blub, blub, swoosh! Down went the tiny lavender fairy and all her stars into the beautiful, clear blue water of the Lake Behind the Pines...and then up she came as she fluttered her wings, up to the surface of the deep blue pond.

Shwoosh once again—as she sputtered and flittered up onto the shore. *Spfft. Ftttss.* "Hoo! That was close!" thought Liddya. "But what a lucky fairy I am. I'm so glad I landed in the Lake Behind the Pines!"

Liddya's stars were all sputtering up out of the lake, too. Sparkle and Twinkle and Glo were shaking and twirling and twinkling to dry off. Spike moved quickly through the sand and grass to tell the others to help Stella dry off. After all, he scolded, she shouldn't have to do it all by herself. Twinkle looked like she was about to cry. She didn't look like she was having fun anymore. Sparkle and Glo moved closer to her to comfort her, and gently wiped off her tiny starpoints. They all lay down on the sand near the lake, drying out in the sun, so glad to be clean and safe.

After a few moments, the stars gathered themselves together and flew up around Liddya just as they always did. They watched her and twittered over her, until she smiled at them and laughed her fairy laugh so they could see that she was okay.

What an adventure! The stars were all sparkly, and Liddya's lavender fairy dress was clean and lavender again, and once again it began to glow.

"Those nice waving pines saved me," she thought. She looked up toward them. She was sure she saw them give her a wink as they rustled and waved in the breeze. She waved her tiny hand to them and blew them a teensy kiss to thank them.

She was sure she heard them whisper in the wind to her, "Take care, little one."

Liddya slowly fluttered around near the lake, drying her wings and her tiny blond curls and her beautiful magic fairy gown.

"Now I know," she thought, "I can cover up with the mud in my tiny house to get past the lumpy bumpy rabbit, and then I can fly to the lake to wash off. I will be free to fly and fly any time I wish, all around the meadow and over the beautiful Lake Behind the Pines."

Liddya was so happy. Her stars were feeling better, too, swirling and twirling all about her in a happy sparkly dance.

Chapter 4

A Wild Ride

One bright sunny day, Liddya and her stars flew around and around the meadow and through the row of waving pines, over the Lake Behind the Pines and back again, all to her heart's content. It was a very good day.

Early in the afternoon, the tiny fairy landed lightly near some wild columbine flowers, admiring their delicate blue blossom faces as they smiled up at the sun. Just then a faraway movement caught her eye. Across the meadow was a furry sleek red fox, with a furry fluffy tail, scampering through the grasses! Liddya fluttered up in the breeze to take a closer look. How fine he was, this sleek red fox! The magical fairy watched him for a while. Then she thought, "How wonderful is this day, with flower faces and foxes and flying for fun!" And with that she flew around and around the meadow again, then through the tall waving pines and over the lake, and back to the sunny meadow with its smiling flower faces.

As she began to settle back among the blossoms, Liddya looked around for the fox and spotted him watching her from across the meadow. Liddya could tell her swirling flight and her sparkling stars had caught the fluffy fox's attention. Before she could stop her flutters, he was right there in the columbine, smiling at her.

"He has a nice smile," she thought, "and such a beautiful fluffy tail!"

She watched as he smiled, and his tail swished this way and that.

"Care to ride on my tail as I run run run?" he said most kindly.

"A ride on your tail?" she thought. "That sounds like fun!"

She fluttered closer and watched the furry tail shift this way and that. This way and that she watched and watched. Then suddenly the red fox turned, first trotting, then running as if to dart away as quickly as he had come! Where was he going?

"I do want a ride!" she thought. So she flew and flew and caught up with the fox as he scampered across the meadow. She reached out her little fairy hands and grabbed for his tail. "Ah! Caught it!" she thought as she held on with all her strength. Liddya's fingers clenched the fluffy foxy tail, and her wings held on, too.

The fox smiled as he glanced back to see her enjoying the ride. "You must love to ride as I run run run," he barked with a smile. Then he peered around and spotted another grassy patch. He turned sharply and ran ran ran.

Over the grasses and through the raspberry patch, past the lumpy bumpy rabbit and around the circle of the wavering pines they went, the furry fox with Liddya holding tight to his fluffy tail.

"Oh, I love the wind in my face," thought the little fairy. Through the breeze she heard a twitter and a twinkle, and looked up to see her tiny stars trying their best to keep up. Just then Twinkle and Stella seemed to give up and fall to the ground. "Oh dear, maybe it's too rough for them, diving through the grasses," thought Liddya as the brushy bushes and pine branches tugged at her lavender gown. But she held on tight to the furry fox's tail as he ran ran ran through the grassy meadow.

Soon Liddya noticed that all the stars had dropped off, and she turned to see them watching her from far behind. "Why do they look so sad?" she wondered. But she was having much too much fun to think about whether she really should leave Spike and Stella, Twinkle and Sparkle and Glo, so she dug her fingers deeper into her new friend's fur so she could go run run running with the wild fox.

"What a ride!" she thought. "Whee!" Liddya and the red fox went all over the land, out of the meadow, beyond the Lake Behind the Pines, into the forest over rocks and boulders and stumps and bumps. "So wonderful!" she thought. "I've never had such a fantastic time!" She hung on to that tail all afternoon.

Finally it was time to go back to her rabbit hole. Liddya wanted very much to do this again someday, but for now she was ready to let go of the furry fox's tail—only she couldn't do it while he was run run running as fast as the wind. But the furry fluffy fox didn't ever stop. He just kept on with his run run running as though he'd forgotten she was even there. She tugged on his tail to get him to look back at her, but he flipped his tail this way and that and ran ran ran up and down and all around. He just...never...stopped!

"Stop!" she thought with all her might. "We have to stop! I want to get off! You've got to stop!"

But the fox didn't even seem to notice her distress.

"What is the matter with you, Mr. Fox? Why do you want to run and run and never stop!?" she thought.

The fox's smile no longer looked nice to her. His red fur no longer felt soft and fluffy. It felt stiff and course. She was afraid! She was getting so hot and so tired. "I have to stop and let go now," she thought. "Stop! Ssstoppp!" she thought even louder.

But the tireless fox was only beginning his wild adventures. "The evening is young," he finally said. "We're just getting warmed up. What is your hurry, little one? Let's have some more fun!" He did not seem to understand why she would want to stop, when there was so much more running to do.

Liddya was so afraid and so tired. Her tiny eyes filled and overflowed with tears. She hung on and hung on for her life with every flip of his tail. Her magical lavender fairy dress was torn and leaking its light.

"What shall I do," she thought. "Oh, what shall I do?" Just then a flick of that foxy tail caught her off guard. Her grasp slipped and her wings let go, and that tail flipped her all the way across the forest. THUD! she landed.

Liddya picked her face up out of the dirt and brushed her tiny curls out of her eyes. "Ohhhh. This was a bad idea," she thought. She looked around her and realized she was far, far away from home. She didn't see a single thing that looked familiar. Worst of all, she did not see her star friends anywhere.

"I am in a scary place very far from my tiny home. What shall I do?" she thought as she watched the red fox seem to get smaller and smaller as he ran further and further away. He ran ran ran through the forest, twitching his tail this way and that, until Liddya could see his smile and his tail no more.

A very quiet and very sad Liddya sat and thought. She was so tired and dirty and so far from home. All she wanted to do was find her way back to her fairy bed, but she didn't even know which way to go. The sun had moved low behind the trees, and there in the dusk she could barely even see past her teensy fairy nose. So much light had leaked out through the rips and tears of her lavender gown, it had only a soft faint glow, like a flickering candle about to go out. Liddya didn't know what else to do, so she found a soft spot in a pile of pine needles and lay down and closed her eyes. The magical lavender fairy fell fast asleep.

Chapter 5

Dragon Dreams

As she dozed in her bed of soft scented pine needles, Liddya dreamed of a big red dragon with a long fiery tail running after her through the pines down the path beside the lake. The dragon had dark spikes along his back, and glowing sparks of fire shot out of his nose and open mouth, lighting the way ahead of him.

With a start, Liddya woke up and sat straight up, her tiny fairy heart pounding in her chest! The sun had set and there was darkness all around her, but she could still see the lighted sparks of the dragon's fire-breathing nose and mouth. The flaming sparks seemed to be lined up in two rows ahead of the dragon. "No, I must not be awake," she thought. "Am I still having a bad dream? But what is the fire I see? Wait—yes, I am awake. The dragon is gone—isn't he?!"

The lavender fairy blinked and blinked. As she peered through the darkness, the sparks from the dragon's nose began to look more like two rows of tiny fairy torches making their way through the forest, flitting and floating between the branches. But—she had never seen such a thing! What could this be? Closer and closer they came. Were they angry fairy soldiers coming to capture her and take her to a dungeon somewhere for abandoning her friends and flying off on the foxy tail? She felt so afraid and sad.

Oh no...they were getting closer. Liddya peered harder through the darkness, trembling in fear. They were nearly right in front of her!

But look! These weren't angry fairy soldiers at all. They were her tiny star friends, each one escorted by a firefly scout! The tiny tails of the fireflies were like glowing green lanterns that never blew out in the breezy night air. And they had come to find her!

"Oh my, oh my! My friends are here!" she thought with delight. "And I treated them so badly. But they're here to take me home!"

Just then the twinkling stars and all the tiny firefly scouts landed in a big circle around Liddya. Stella twittered over and introduced Liddya to the chief firefly scout, Captain Luminus. Stella explained how she'd met the scouts as they worked in the meadow, lighting the way to guide a young frog family home after dark. When the scouts had heard Stella's story of Liddya's dangerous ride on the furry fox, they all flew into formation and charged ahead, following Stella and her sparkling little friends to find this mysterious adventurous fairy.

The tiny stars swarmed and swirled around Liddya, happy to be reunited with their lavender mud fairy friend. Sparkle and Twinkle held her torn lavender gown together so Glo could reconnect its lights. But there was only so much the little star could do out there in the middle of nowhere in the middle of the night. "It's just fine, Glo," Liddya thought. "I don't mind if it leaks a bit of light here and there. I just want to go home."

So one by one the tiny fairy stars and all the firefly scouts lined up on either side of Liddya and prepared to guide her through the forest and across the meadow, safely back to her tiny home in the tiny rabbit hole beside the raspberry patch.

Stella glowed and led the way, flying and fluttering her starry eyes at a handsome firefly scout, the one with the brightest, most wonderful glow in his tail. Spike knocked the poor surprised scout out of the way to fly next to Stella. They all fluttered dizzily through the forest, making their way home, over the fields of tall grasses, above the rocks and boulders, stumps and bumps, through the waving pines, into the dark night sky.

WHEN THEY WERE FINALLY near the raspberry patch Stella had been describing to Captain Luminus along the way, the shiny little star pointed down toward the rabbit hole that was home to the adventurous little fairy and her star friends. The firefly scouts stopped and hovered in two rows, saluting Liddya and the stars as though guarding them while they dipped and swooshed past the umbrella tree where the lumpy rabbit surely must be. Liddya really,

really hoped he was sleeping! She was much too tired to think about getting thumped or bumped before she could finally make it home to her very own bed.

But the rabbit was nowhere to be seen, so into the cozy rabbit hole flew Liddya and all her stars, back into their tiny home all safe and sound.

Liddya was so glad to be alive and safe in her tiny house. She and all the stars made one last trip up to the top of the rabbit hole so they could wave goodbye to the brave firefly ranger scouts.

Captain Luminus held his salute. "Happy to help!" he said.

"Thank you!" waved Liddya.

Stella blew tiny star kisses.

Chapter 6

A New Friend

Liddya spent the next morning in her little house, cleaning up the mud and reconnecting with her tiny star friends. Overnight, her magical lavender fairy gown seemed to have repaired itself as good as new. Liddya wondered if Glo had secretly helped. Or was that just what magical gowns are known to do in times like these...?

"I am finished with adventures," she thought. "I'm staying home where it is safe. I love my little rabbit hole and I am happy here." She twirled and she flew...but she could only fly in tiny circles, for her little home was so very small.

All that afternoon Liddya sat and thought...and thought some more. Mostly she thought about the lumpy bumpy rabbit. She thought he surely must have seen them all drag in last evening in such a ragged condition, flying into the rabbit hole. Why didn't he come to thump and bump them before they made it into their home? Did the firefly scouts scare him away? Or maybe he really had been asleep…? Anyway, she was so glad he hadn't thumped her after such a long tired day of adventure.

And then the tiny fairy looked up at the small round light way up high in the ceiling. "I have an idea," she thought. She gathered her tiny sparkling star friends and told them what she had in mind. They all nodded and sparkled together, and agreed that it most certainly was the right thing to do.

All together the lavender mud fairy and her tiny sparkly stars flew to the entrance of the rabbit hole. Sure enough, there sat the lumpy ol' bumpy ol' rabbit in the raspberry patch, watching the entryway. When he saw Liddya watching him, he looked at her with his very big whiskery scowl. Liddya was afraid he might want to give her a final thump and be done with it. He certainly did not look happy to see her again.

But Liddya and all her tiny stars pretended not to notice. They took a long run and a giant leap out the door, flying low, directly toward the lumpy bumpy rabbit.

"What...are you doing?" the rabbit sneered. "Have you completely lost your mind, you irritating little fairy?! I'll swat you with one of my strong thumping legs, and that will be the end of you!" the angry rabbit snorted.

Liddya, accompanied by her squadron of stars, made a beeline directly for that old rabbit, and in one sparkly swoop they flew right under his fluffy white pom-pom tail, and swooshed up beneath him. The stars swirled around, just as they had planned, on all sides of the tiny fairy, who with all her might lifted that lumpy bumpy rabbit up into the sky to take him for the spin of his life!

Over the meadow, between the tall, waving pines, around the Lake Behind the Pines, and into the forest they carried him. The lumpy bumpy rabbit hung on to the little fairy and her tiny stars for dear life, his big bumpy paws trembling as he held on with all his might.

"You're going to kill me!" the rabbit cried out.

"Just wait, lumpy rabbit," Liddya said out loud. "Let us show you just how much fun a lumpy rabbit can have!"

"I know you're trying to get rid of me for all the thumping I did! You're going to drop me out of the sky and that will be the end of me. Oh, woe is me. Oh, woe is me! Let me down now!"

But the tiny fairy just giggled and said, "Isn't this fun, lumpy bumpy rabbit?!" She was sure he must be having as much fun flying as she always did.

The stars all twittered with glee as they danced and swirled the bumpy rabbit all over creation.

Finally Liddya and the stars brought the grumpy old rabbit back to the raspberry patch, gently setting him down.

As he let himself crumple limply to the ground, the lumpy bumpy rabbit looked surprised and relieved. He sat shaking quietly, watching the lavender fairy. "Why were you so careful with me, little magical fairy? You could have dropped me into the lake, and that would have been the end of me. But even though I have thumped you and tried to get rid of you, you decided to bring me safely back to my raspberry patch...?"

The little magical fairy smiled a real smile and said aloud, "I want to be your friend, lumpy bumpy rabbit. I wanted to share my fun with you! You never get to fly or go away from here. So I thought it was time to share with you my most favorite thing to do."

The lumpy rabbit got tears in his big brown eyes. "No one has ever wanted to be my friend before," he told Liddya. "Ever since my kind old lumpy bumpy mother was snatched away by a huge shaggy wolf late one evening a long time ago, when I was very young and small, I have been afraid to go far from this little rabbit hole, even though I have now grown too big to live there anymore." He confessed to Liddya that he had hated her for living in the house that he and his mother had once called home. "I have missed my mother so much," he told his new friends.

But now he actually had friends! So Liddya and her stars and the lumpy bumpy rabbit all formed a circle around the old tree stump, and danced and sang about their new friendship and fun adventures. Liddya invited the lumpy bumpy rabbit to a picnic with their yummy creamy soup and polka dotted candy sticks, and they all agreed that was an excellent idea.

AND FROM THAT DAY ON, Liddya and her stars and the lumpy bumpy rabbit all lived together at the edge of the meadow near the raspberry patch, happily ever after. The tiny magical lavender mud fairy and her teensy sparkly star friends flew and flew each and every day, here and there and around and about, to many places they had never seen before. But they always returned to their little home at the bottom of the old rabbit hole, for that was the place they loved the very most. Sometimes they invited the grumpy rabbit (who really wasn't grumpy any more) to fly with them, but he always decided to stay on the ground. He thanked Liddya and the stars very much, but said he never ever wanted to fly again.

So Liddya and her stars flew and flew, and the lumpy bumpy rabbit stayed in the raspberry patch near the overgrown juniper bush. And there was never any reason for any of them to use mud to hide their light or their sparkles—or their lumps—ever again.

The End.

About the Author

Linda P. Geiger, M.H.I., R.N., B.S.N., C.N.O.R., is a registered nurse, university professor, life coach, and professional speaker who makes her home in the Colorado Rockies. She has lived and traveled throughout the United States and in Africa as a Chief Operations Officer and consultant for global healthcare organizations.

The story of *The Lavender Mud Fairy* came to life at a writing camp she attended in Hawaii, with ties to characters and events in her Montana childhood. The story of friendship, adventures, and letting one's true light shine is written to inspire children in their development of courage, imagination, and self-esteem.

For more information about Linda and
her work, visit her website at
www.MiraclesEveryMoment.com.

Made in the USA
Las Vegas, NV
17 December 2021

38417320R00040